THE FRIENDLY ADVENTURES
OF THE
Georgia Blue Flower Truck

Written by Gina Dzierzanowski
Illustrated by QBN Studios

gatekeeper press
Columbus, Ohio

The Friendly Adventures of the Georgia Blue Flower Truck

Published by Gatekeeper Press
2167 Stringtown Rd., Suite 109
Columbus, OH 43123-2989
www.GatekeeperPress.com

The cover design, interior formatting, illustrations and typesetting for this book are entirely the product of the author. Gatekeeper Press did not participate in and is not responsible for any aspect of these elements.

Library of Congress Control Number: 2021950272

ISBN (hardcover): 9781662921957
ISBN (paperback): 9781662921964
eISBN: 9781662921971

This book is dedicated to the two people
I love more than words can express.

To my husband, for your love and commitment
to me, you are the most supportive, encouraging,
and loving man in the entire universe.
You give me the security to soar.

To my ridiculously smart, kind, and beautiful
daughter who is every beat of my heart.
You inspire me to be the best that I can be.

I love you both so much; you are my world.

Acknowledgements

With the deepest gratitude, I would like to thank the many people who have helped make the Georgia Blue Flower Truck so successful in such a short amount of time. Some I have known my entire life and others I've met through this journey. All of you have inspired, touched, and illuminated me through your presence.

First and foremost, I would like to express my love and gratitude to my mom, dad, and sister for their never-ending support, and for generously sharing their love and wisdom.

To ALL in the Hudson Valley community who have welcomed the Georgia Blue Flower Truck, with special acknowledgments to:

Meadowbrook Farm, who was the very first local business to welcome the Georgia Blue Flower Truck into Wappingers Falls, New York.

Evelyn, the owner of the Hudson Valley Wreath Company-- thank you for selflessly introducing and sharing your business community with me.

Danielle & Veronica, owners of Hudson Square Boutique for generously sharing your customers with the Georgia Blue Flower Truck at so many wonderful events.

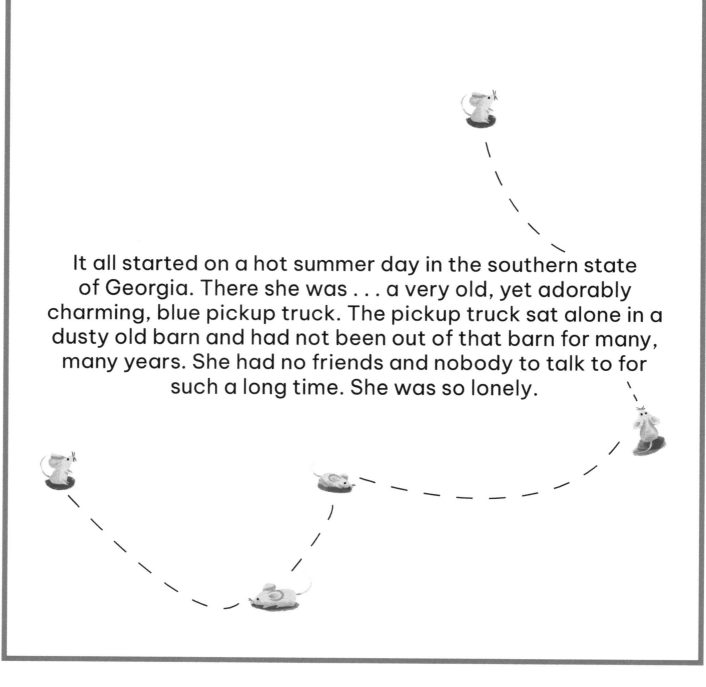

It all started on a hot summer day in the southern state of Georgia. There she was . . . a very old, yet adorably charming, blue pickup truck. The pickup truck sat alone in a dusty old barn and had not been out of that barn for many, many years. She had no friends and nobody to talk to for such a long time. She was so lonely.

One day a curious young lady named Julia opened the doors to the barn. Julia took one look at the truck and knew that this pickup truck was ready for some fun adventures.

Julia dusted off the pickup truck. She opened the door, got in, started the engine, rolled down the windows and smiled as she drove off. The pickup truck was finally free and very happy to be out of that dusty old barn.

As she drove down the beautiful country roads, Julia decided that this adorable truck needed a catchy name and a wonderful purpose. She decided that she would make this truck the most special truck ever. She would make it a truck that spreads love and happiness everywhere it goes.

Julia decided that she would make the truck a beautiful flower truck. The flower truck would bring the most lovely flowers to people in different neighborhoods. It would be one-of-a-kind. Now, the only thing left to do was find the perfect name for her truck.

Julia passed a flower field and decided to stop to have a picnic. While she was having her picnic, she thought of names for her flower truck. She said a bunch of names aloud but none of them sounded right. She thought about where she was . . . Georgia. She looked around, then she looked at the blue truck, and BOOM! That was it! She figured out the most perfect name-- the Georgia Blue Flower Truck!

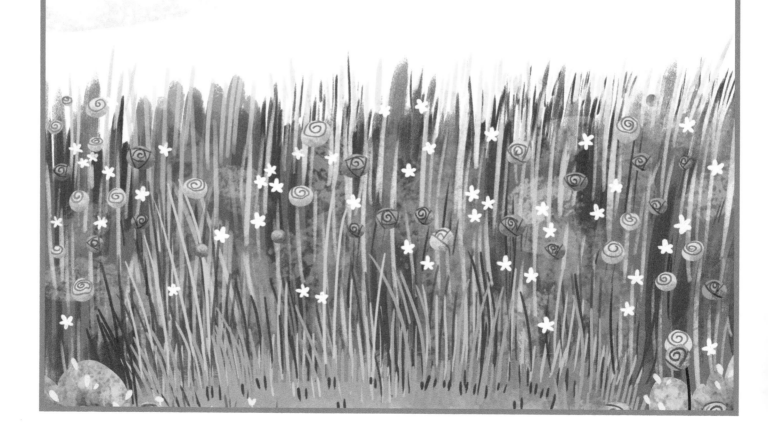

Now that Julia had chosen the name for her flower truck it was time for her to hang a bunch of old tin buckets on both sides of the truck to hold the beautiful flowers.

With the buckets hung on the Georgia Blue Flower Truck, it was time for Julia to pick some flowers. She drove to the flower farm and chose many different types of flowers. Some of the flowers Julia picked were tulips, daisies, roses and sunflowers.

After the flowers were picked, Julia put them into the buckets on each side of the Georgia Blue Flower Truck. She was ready to find the most perfect spot to park to sell her beautiful flowers.

Julia drove around town for a while looking for the most perfect spot to park the Georgia Blue Flower Truck. Finally, she spotted a parking lot in front of a very cute toy store and clothing boutique.

"This is perfect!" Julia said. "I hope they will let me park here to sell flowers."

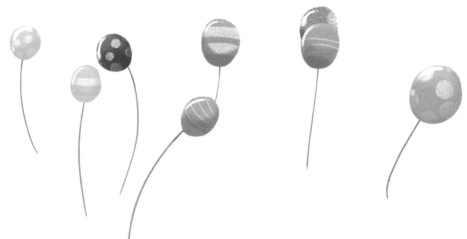

As Julia pulled into the parking lot, she realized there were many people looking out the windows at them. The entire neighborhood was excited to see the flower truck. She hadn't even had a chance to park and already people couldn't wait to see this wonderful truck filled with beautiful flowers.

Two ladies came out from the boutique, wanting to see the beautiful truck, and they asked Julia if she could stay and sell flowers in front of their store. Julia smiled and happily said, "YESSS!! Thank you both so much. I was so worried I would not have a place to sell my beautiful flowers."

Julia started setting up the flower truck. She made sure that all the flowers were perfectly placed and looked their very best. Julia thought to herself, *What if nobody shows up to buy my flowers?*

She started to feel VERY sad and worried.

Suddenly, Julia heard a small voice. It was a little girl with her mommy. The little girl said "Excuse me, please don't look so sad. I'd like to buy some flowers."

Julia jumped up with a smile and said, "Welcome to the Georgia Blue Flower Truck, you can choose any flowers you'd like!"

Once the little girl chose her flowers, Julia wrapped them up in a beautiful bouquet at the back of the truck. She told the little girl how much she appreciated her buying her flowers; she would never forget that she was her very first customer.

When Julia looked up after handing the little girl her bouquet, she could not believe her eyes. There was a line wrapped around the Georgia Blue Flower Truck. It looked like the entire neighborhood had shown up to support Julia's first day out.

Now that Julia had so many customers, she was hard at work and busy as a bee! She wrapped so many cheerful bouquets for everyone in the neighborhood. Everyone was happy!! People were even taking pictures with Georgia Blue.

With the help of two generous boutique owners and supportive neighbors in the community, the Georgia Blue Flower Truck turned out to be exactly what Julia had wished for--a flower truck spreading love and happiness everywhere it goes.

"See you all on our next adventure!" Julia yelled as she got back into Georgia Blue.

About the Author

Gina Dzierzanowski is an up-and-coming children's book author and a published poet. Gina's newest writings are her children's book series "The Friendly Adventures of The Georgia Blue Flower Truck," based on the stories encountered while running her charming flower truck business. Gina was born and raised in Westchester County, New York, and now resides in Dutchess County, New York, with her husband and daughter. Gina strives to make small businesses more successful by fostering a close networking team approach amongst small and local businesses.

Follow Georgia Blue Flower truck on instagram @georgiablueflowertruck for all updates about the Georgia Blue Flower Truck.

About Illustrators

QBN Studios is a small Illustration studio located in Vernon, Connecticut. Owners Quynh Nguyen and Christopher MacCoy are passionate about helping authors fulfill their dreams, and bring their words to life. QBN Studio's goal is to create an immersive experience for their audiences to tumble headfirst into imaginary worlds. Follow us on Instagram @qbnstudios for the latest updates on illustrations, books, and other projects.

CPSIA information can be obtained
at www.ICGtesting.com
Printed in the USA
LVHW071101200422
716702LV00003B/3

9 781662 921964